SONFLOWER SUBMISSION

Pride may cause a fall,
but humility brings honor.

Proverbs 29:23

D1522410

DeVeria Gore

ISBN 978-1-63575-778-1 (Paperback)
ISBN 978-1-63575-779-8 (Digital)

Christian Faith Publishing, Inc.
296 Chestnut Street
Meadville, PA 16335
www.christianfaithpublishing.com

Printed in the United States of America

I dedicate this book to my Lord, Jesus Christ, who is
the head of my family who also share in this tribute!
You all amaze me!

Thanks be to God, His Son, and the Holy Spirit who are
the story of the ages! It was on their hearts that this story should
come to pass. Thank You Lord for nudging me to tell Your
story, and I am honored to have been given the blessing that
this has become *Our Story*.

I also thank my husband, Ed, of 41 years who checked on
me often and encouraged me when I was not writing, or called
me away when I had been writing for hours. You have amazing
patience and I love how you take such good care of me!

A big thank you to my daughter, *Ashley*, sisters, *Denise
and Debra*, and church friend, *Kim G.*, who read much, or all,
of this story and gave real feedback to me. I appreciate your
sincerity and encouragement. Thank you!

And to my son, *Austin*, my parents, my pastors, other
family members and friends who always said, "You can do this,"
thank you so much for your prayers and for believing in me!

To you, dear reader, I praise God for your
support of this new author,
and I pray blessing upon you and your
family as you read these pages
filled with the realities of pride's stubborn heart in the presence
of the Lord's submitted heart!
May He minister to you as He has ministered to me!

Goodbye pride, hello submission!

CONTENTS

PREFACE

One morning, on my way to work, a row of sunflowers caught my eye as I passed by. I was struck by how bent they were. They seemed to be in total submission to something...someone. Despite their tremendous height, they bowed. Despite their plate-size power blooms, they bowed as no other flower I had ever seen.

Over the next several months, I followed their life's course noticing how they became dry, drier, and finally, dead; yet the fascinating thing was that even in the shell-of-a-flower state, they remained bowed. Before God, I began to wonder about how much bowing I do in the midst of frustrations, irritations, and hardships. Not that much, I'm afraid, and the reason is because of one strong little aspect of my character called *pride*. If you have never been visited by a bit of seasoned pride yourself, then perhaps you should spend your dollar on another book, but for many of us, pride has been a lurking culprit responsible for stealing some of the best treasures we could ever know. God wants to bless us, and it is not always the enemy who is standing in the way. Oftentimes, pride is the guilty trickster.

As you read this tale of how the sunflower learns to submit to the Master Gardener, I pray that you are blessed into a realm of living that loosens your control and causes you to yield all the more to our loving Savior's plan for our lives. So, exit pride; enter submission.

INTRODUCTION

After all things were made by Him who is the Creator, a garden was fashioned to house Man and Choice. Choice offered Man both the opportunity for Good with the option for Evil. Man, whom Creator loved, could choose freely. Creator's heart was toward Man—His hope was that Man would choose Good, for Good's parents were named Life. Evil's relatives were named Death. To receive eternal Life, all Man had to do was submit to Creator. Man, however, was tricked by Evil's cousin, Liar. Liar said that if Man chose Evil, he would be like Creator and would never die. That thought touched Pride in Man. Man listened and Pride pondered on this. Could it be that he could actually become as wonderful as Creator!

Then Man felt Confusion, for he had always heard that Man would live forever with Creator if he only believed in Him. Well, Man's Pride believed Liar and finally chose Evil to be his new friend. When Evil took Man's hand, Shame appeared. It was not long before Guilt showed up also, and Man came to know Sorrow and Sadness. Even Sickness and Murder visited Man...and the heart of Creator grieved.

What must I do to help the proud Man, wondered Creator, *for even now, I love him.* Creator thought for a moment and immediately decided, *I'll send My Son to Man! Yes, and if Man will submit to Him, we can be family still! My Son will show Man how to silence Pride, how to hear Truth. Man will learn how to defeat the Evil One by the example of My Son, and finally, Man will know Deep Joy, Peace and Utter Contentment. This will be My gift—the gift of a second Chance. If only Man will submit...*

CHAPTER ONE

Falling: Dropped and Dying

Falling, falling, I land on my back in a hollow black spot. After resting a moment, I feel black snow come floating down on my hot face. I've gotta get out of here, but I don't see a way big enough. There is still a little light though through those openings above, but now what? Oh, it's so dark down here, and what's this? Warm? Ugh, let me hush. I hear someone near me.

"Who's there?" I call out.

"My name is Son. Who are you?"

"Name's Priden. Not sure I should be telling you that since I don't really know you and all. Who are you and what are you doing down here? What's the way out and…"

"Wait, wait! Not so fast," Son interrupts. "We have plenty of time to get to know each other. Why are you in such a hurry? There's really lots and lots of time."

"That's easy for you to say maybe, but the way I see it, we need to get going." Priden pauses, but then resumes, "And the sooner, the better. Look, I've never been down here before, but you can bet I'm finding a way out *right now!*"

"Where must you be right now?" asked Son.

"Well, you know, I have people to see, things to do, and just…uh, why am I explaining this to you? What did you say your name is?"

"Son, my name is Son."

"Well Son, I just need to get back to my stuff. You know, my things. Let's face it. This is a dark place down here, although I have been in dark places before, you know.

Anyway, the real problem is I didn't ask to come here! How dare the Gardener just drop me off like that! He didn't even ask what I thought about all this! The nerve of that One!" fumed Priden.

"Well, I asked to come here," commented Son. "I heard about how dark places can begin to have light if we wish for it to be so."

"Yeah, and you're not thinking straight. Although, there are a few light places peeking through above us. Anyway, all I need is a plan. I'll think of something. I always do. I can trust me when I can't trust anyone else, so see ya later. I'm going to be busy for a while," Priden added.

Son looked calmly toward Priden's space, wondering how long it would be before Priden realized he did not have the resources to meet this challenge. Escape would come, but not in the way Priden was accustomed to seeing.

Son pushed deeper into the warmth of his little spot, making Himself comfortable. Rest fell gently upon Him as time inched by like a worm. Soon, Son was asleep.

In Priden's area, thinking and mumbling were going on. Lots of it. He even wondered how Son could sleep at a time like this. After all, didn't Son know they could actually die down here in this powder jungle? How could He be so calm! Priden busied himself with shifting his weight from one side to the other in his shell. Nothing moved around him. No path appeared either. If only there were something to climb so he could get out, get free. Son might even want to come with him.

Then he heard it: a sound, tumbling and skipping through the blackness. He shushed himself and waited. There it was again! *No, it can't be*, he thought, but sure enough there it was, the sound of laughter—a female's laughter! *Whoever she is, she had better not be laughing at me*, he thought. The laughter happened again. This time, he could tell the direction it came from—sort of to the right of Son's spot it seemed.

Silence. Then…

"Ah, there it is again," exclaimed Priden. "Hello over there," he yelled. "What's so funny, whoever you are?"

"Oops! I told Wind not to play around so! She keeps belching bubbles all over the place. Something got her stirred up today and she has been twirling around ever since." The laughing voice paused, and then exclaimed, "Oh my, I'm just carrying on like a woodpecker! Ah, you asked my name?"

"Not really, but okay, who are you?" Priden asked again.

"My name is Deep Joy and what might your happy name be?" she inquired.

"I don't know about happy, but they call me Priden. Right now I'm trying to work my way out of this darkness. I can't stand it down here. There's nothing to do, nothing to see, and

I've only met one other being so far. His Name is Son. You'd laugh if you knew what He was doing right now."

"What?" Deep Joy asked. "Swinging in a hammock?"

"Well, yes, sort of! He is sleeping! How did you know? Wow, you should see Him. It's like He doesn't even care about being down here. Clearly he's not worried about being uncomfortable, sick, dying, or well anything," Priden informed her. "Of course, I'm not worried either. Just so you know, I'm really working on a plan to save us all." Frowning, he commented, "I still can't get over Master Gardener doing this to me though, but He must have thrown you and Son down here too, Deep Joy. How else would you have landed in such a place?"

Deep Joy let out a light, musical giggle. "Well, actually," she began, "I was in His hand just yesterday when Wind began to dance wildly across the sky. I delighted so in the dance that I began to laugh and squeal. When Wind noticed me laughing, she swooped down and tickled me. I laughed so hard that I flipped right out of Master Gardener's hand! Wind let me surf in her hair until I landed in this black powder place. I looked way up and asked Master Gardener if He could pick me up. He said yes, but that it would be later when He returned for me. Then He patted the place above me and I knew I was forgiven for rushing things a bit. Then I just laughed inside for comfort."

Priden was glad Deep Joy couldn't see the smirk on his face. How could this jolly one not understand the danger they were all in? Finally, he threw this remark at her, "Well, that's nice for you, but I'm plowing a trail out of here! There's no way I'm rotting down here inside of Nowhere!"

"Listen to me Priden. I know He's coming back for me because He's never left me or forsaken me. And Priden, you know what?" asked Deep Joy.

"No, what?" Priden threw the question into space.

"He hasn't left you either."

Priden loaded, aimed, and fired back, "Well, you're wrong about that! He knew I wanted no part in this, but He got rid of me without so much as a comment! Even if He does come back for you, He won't be back for me. But then, you know what? I don't need Him to come back!" Priden blinked and swallowed hard trying to believe his own words.

"Yes you do, Priden. We all do. Let me introduce you to someone else down here."

"What! There are others down here?" he asked in disbelief.

"Yes, many others, but I want you to meet someone who is very special. He's a kind friend of mine and he loves when no else can. He's on the other side of Son. Just a minute. Let me get his attention."

"Meek! Oh Meeeeek! Meek, are you listening? It's me, Deep Joy," she sang.

A gentle voice entered the darkness from just to the left of Son. "Oh, hi Deep Joy. It's been a while. How are you?" he inquired.

"Great and getting better. There's someone that I want you to meet. He's curious and interesting. Meek, I'm introducing you to Priden. Priden, meet my buddy, Meek."

Their hellos butted into each other and Meek graciously allowed Priden to express himself first. "How's it going man? Is your name really Meek? I've never heard of a name quite like that, or is it short for something else?" Priden asked.

"No, my name really is Meek and I'm pleased to meet you Priden. Everyone calls me Meek. It's short and easy, to the point, I guess you could say."

"Yeah, to the point. Speaking of the *point*, I'm working on a plan, but since you are one of the 'lucky' souls to be trapped down here, you may have some ideas already lined up on how to escape. Care to share some of them Meek, 'cause the way I see it, we need to be heading out of here real soon. How 'bout it?" asked Priden.

Meek looked towards Deep Joy's spot wondering if she knew more about Priden. He seemed like a likable fellow and he must want to fit in well, but why was he insisting on working on *plans*? What could he hope to accomplish with plans of his own? Not wanting the silence to label him as rude, Meek made Priden an offer. "Priden, I want you to know that I have no plans or thoughts for how to get out of here. It is certain that this has been taken care of by One greater than me. However, I do offer you times to talk. Whenever you get lonesome, please, just call out and we can talk those moments away," suggested Meek.

"Lonesome?! I don't get lonely! I'm perfectly content all by myself. Good to hear that you're concerned, but I can manage on my own, Meek. I, for one, don't intend to stay down here another day in a nowhere place, doing absolutely nothing for no one in particular! The *plan* is to get *me* out of here! Got it?"

"I'm so sorry you think that way," replied Meek. "Sounds like you're feeling a bit of frustration and perhaps you're a little afraid all at the same time? Maybe I can help you with that," Meek offered.

Darkness covered the most evil frown in the land as Priden retorted, "How dare you act like you know my feelings! You just met me and I've said no such thing! Watch your brainy mouth, Meek! You may mean well, but you don't know one shred of info about me, not one shred!" snapped Priden.

Meek waited and let stillness swallow Priden's words out of the grains of powder. When he spoke, it was soft and gentle. "You're right. I have no right to analyze your words. It's just that, though I hear your words, I also hear your heart and I once said words very similar to yours. It took the Master Gardener and His Crew to change my heart," Meek reported.

"Well, nothing and no one needs to change me. I'm perfectly fine just the way I am. I do all the right things and I'm not saying that's been easy, but I've been fairly successful on my own, thank you! So, I don't need your advice! Save it for the other poor souls trapped down here."

"No, you don't need my advice," replied Meek. "Wow, it's getting late. The light places above have gotten gray and we must rest now. Rest is our next step. Perhaps I'll get to chat with you again. I'm glad we met Priden. You are one of great promise."

Relaxing some, Priden admitted, "Sure, it is late and it was okay meeting you too, Meek. I'm going to think a while longer on my escape plan. Somebody's got to do it—might as well be me. I'll let you know what I come up with. You might want to get out of here sooner rather than later."

"Yes, I'm told there is a large inheritance waiting for me, so yes, I do want to leave here someday. I just know that Master Gardener has the blue print for that." He sighed peacefully and added, "Goodnight Priden, my friend."

"Goodnight, Meek," called Priden and then he added, "Goodnight, Deep Joy."

Smiling sweetly, Deep Joy whispered back, "Goodnight Priden."

Son dreamed of all the happiness yet to come. The next day, faint light began to illuminate the powder. Blackness warmed and roused Son who stretched wide and pierced the darkness with the root that would establish Him forever. The death of sleep was thrown off like a blanket and life leaped to the scene showing the others the way to move up. It would be in the pushing down that upward progress could be made.

Across the way, Priden snored loud and strong. Dirt plans rested at his side, limp and useless. It had been very late when he finally gave in to rest. Exhaustion was the only signal to which he bowed. It was clear that thinking would have to wait for tomorrow.

And then, suddenly, liquid was moving everywhere. No one had put in a request for it, but here it was, mushy, wet, and uncontrolled. It wrapped itself around every particle of powder and every deposit in the cradle of blackness. No place was missed. Deep Joy was roused from her slumber by it and had to regain her balance. She did so quickly though, for she had been here long enough to be accustomed to these wet times; some were more drenching than others.

It was an odd pattern, yes, but something good was happening. You came in dry, then you were warmed a bit, only to be soaked and allowed to nearly dry out again. What a cycle, but what softening was happening too. Deep Joy had noticed that Son was softened days ago and had actually split to allow the arm to be extended that would tap into life springs. His shell was gently falling away.

Wow, she chuckled to herself. *Son died quickly. His outer self just gave in on His own free will. I'll be able to do the same soon,* she hoped.

Just then, she remembered Priden! Priden would never like this situation. Whatever plan he had percolating would never include getting soaked. *He must be exhausted,* she thought, *because I only hear snoring over there. Somehow his shell may be a lot tougher and thicker so it may take many, many soakings to achieve what Son so easily has done—die to self."*

In a whisper so as not to disturb Priden, Deep Joy tried to get Meek's attention.

"Meek! *Pst*! Meek! Are you awake," she called.

"Of course, Deep Joy. I'm enjoying my bath time. Being bathed in the Master Gardener's solution is one of my most enjoyable moments for existing."

Deep Joy piped in, "I remember how you used to grumble though about the baths. You never even liked a quick rinsing."

"I don't mind it at all now because I understand what it is for, and mainly, who it is from. I trust Master Gardener. He knows me better than I know myself and He has thought of everything. Why, He's never allowed the waters to rise above me even though the water was all around me. His awesome light kept me from drowning each and every time," explained Meek.

"Yes, He has thought of everything," agreed Deep Joy.

Priden startled them both with, "Who's thought of everything? What are you two whispering about?"

"Oh Priden, sorry we disturbed your rest. We didn't mean to talk so," added Meek.

"Well, what were you saying anyway?" inquired Priden. "Any word on what this mushy stuff is all around us? My goodness, I can hardly breathe! I feel all weighted down, pressure on every side. I can't even move!"

"Oh Priden," waned Meek, "this is the beginning of a process called soaking, a *bath* if you will."

"A bath? But I'm clean as a whistle. I never get dirty. Good guy awards come to me nearly all the time. Not even your grandma could wish for a better chap if I were her grandkid!"

"Priden, listen. We all have gotten messy and fallen short of the Master Gardener's love. Don't you know that? By now, you should be soft enough to take root right where you are, but there's still a degree of…if you'll pardon me, firmness. Stubbornness and brittleness can only be relieved by the soakings," Meek gently added.

Priden fumed in the moist darkness. He began to tremble with anger, and with the greatest effort, he shook as much moisture away from himself as he possibly could. Some slid off but, not content with this, he heaved again causing more to roll back into the darkness.

"There," he said as if to applaud his accomplishment. "I'll have nothing to do with any soakings, drenchings, or wettings of any kind! I'm fine just the way I am. No one tells me how or when to change. I call the shots on that, got it?" he yelled. Priden stared into nothing, listened and heard the same—nothing.

"*Hmph*! Don't want to talk, heh? Well, that's fine too! All this talk of soakings has gotten me off track. I've got to get back to my escape plans. Let's see, where are they? They must be tucked on this side of me," he mused leaning to his right just a bit.

Then a faint whisper reached out to him. Priden stopped moving. When he heard silence, he continued gathering his master plan and busied himself musing over how to proceed from where he had left off. Suddenly, the whisper came again and echoed around him, almost moving through him.

"Wow, who's there?" Priden managed to ask.

The clear response came back: "I love you and in softness I fell here to die for you. Soon I will get up with all power in My hand. You shall know Me and My Father. You shall delight in Me and know My way. Great will be our time together—only submit."

Instantly, a clap of thunder blasted the ground and rocked its way from one side of the dark to the other. In the quiet that followed, real liquid began moving everywhere. Before long, it had moved into every space, forming a black ocean. In no time, it found Meek and Deep Joy, and sure enough, flowed over and around Priden smooth and slick-like.

"Oh my goodness! I am toast, cooked meat, and fried apples!! What have I done? I'm in a terrible mess now, one I might not be able to fix, but oh, I've got to try. I have *got to try*," shrieked Priden.

"Let go, Priden!" It was Meek again. "Just relax and let go! There is but one way out and this begins the journey. Let go. It was Son speaking to you a moment ago. He and Master Gardener are preparing you for a beautiful passage. It might not be what you planned, but it is truly the way and the life. Anyone who follows it will surely live. Just let go."

"I can't. Look at all the work I've done on my escape idea! I'm proud of my work. This idea could bring me great fortune, for others would certainly buy it for times such as these. Gosh, if I can just manage to stay dry," he squirmed in protest.

Deep Joy could stand it no longer, so she chimed in, "Priden, you think goodness and works are everything. Directly behind you are the remains of a good soul who never recognized Son's or Master Gardener's love. He called himself Goody. He was polite, hardworking, and even gave of himself to support others who were less fortunate. Then he decided to resist the touch of the Master Gardener. No moisture touched him, no light, no word. It wasn't long before he crumbled and was left to dissolve away."

"Aha! See! The soakings couldn't save him!" retorted Priden.

"Yes, but they could have if he hadn't resisted. You see, he cut himself off from the rest of us. He inched his way over far enough that he became wedged under a rock. That's too hard of a place for soakings to be effective, and he dried up and crumbled. It was so slow and painful. We could hear the sound of his agony for days. It would have been better if he had been instantly crushed."

"Oh no! What a horrible way to lose life," said Priden.

"Yes, especially since he had no way to gain it back," added Deep Joy.

"You mean there's a way to gain life back once it's gone?" Priden asked stunned.

"Absolutely, Priden. That's the Master Gardener's plan. We submit to His Son and though we were dead, yet shall we live!" [John 11:14] "Dying is but a sleeping, a long nap from which we can be raised into the newness of life. Son is here to show us how—He is our great example."

"Why look to Son, though? We can't even see Him," questioned Priden.

"That's just it Priden. The less we see, the better off we are. It's about *faith*. We believe without seeing and are rewarded for our blind faith for now. Later, there will be a point in which we will see him fully, face to face, but for now, we trust with unflinching belief."

"Hmmm," moaned Priden.

"Think about it Priden…it's like not seeing the wind, but knowing exactly when it blows. Blind faith—just know it's there—use your heart to see, not your eyes. Sometimes the eyes tell you things that are not true. We see one thing, but assume something else. Believe with your spirit and know that *truth* will happen."

"Yeah, kind of like hearing your voice, but not seeing you. I know you're there; you do exist. I hear you, but can't touch you…or see you. Is that it?"

"That's it Priden! Just let go."

"Let go, as in *stop*?"

"Yes. Just stop everything."

"But what if my plan might be better, or easier? What if I could have a quicker solution? How about…"

Deep Joy interrupted, "There are no 'what ifs' Priden. There's just being still and knowing that the Master Gardener is in control."

"But I thought I could be in control. I'm good at that. What's wrong with *me* being in charge?" asked Priden seriously wanting to know.

"Look, Priden, we think too small when we start talking about being in charge. Did you know that Master Gardener always wanted us to subdue the earth and have dominion over everything in it?" [Gen. 1: 27-28]

"No. I wasn't thinking of being *that* 'in charge'! I like just running my own business, my own affairs. You know, just keeping order all around *me*."

"Well, Master Gardener wants you to let Him bring total order. Long ago, Master Gardener gave two of us total authority over a place called the Garden of Eden. It was the first and finest garden in the Earth. Then an evil one convinced the chosen two to pick Death rather than Life. For this, the two had to be dismissed from the Garden. Afterwards, many were born in the Earth who tried to do Good, but Evil kept showing up. Master Gardener has now sent Son for us to believe in so that we can become joint heirs with Him over not just a garden, but joint heirs over *all* the Earth. Now that's being in charge, Priden."

"Yeah, I guess you're right," Priden reflected, "but I'm not comfortable with just dropping everything. It all sounds good, but I don't want to, you know, lose myself," he whispered.

"It's uncomfortable when it's your first time Priden, but Master Gardener desires that none be lost. In fact, He's seen to it that all the ones who lose their lives for His sake, will always find them again." [Matt. 16:25] "The one, though, who holds onto his life, or himself, will ultimately lose himself," explained Deep Joy.

"What? How can I be lost and found at the same time?" squeaked Priden. "What kind of sense does that make?"

"Why, it makes perfect sense," she chuckles. "It's Son who does the great finding. He picks us up and dusts us off. Then He reveals His plan for us so we can fulfill our destiny. Outside of Him, we are lost—nothing. Apart from Him, we can do nothing of any real consequence. The work is done by Him through us—we simply surrender. We stop. We yield to Him, and things begin to happen. He increases, but we reap the benefit of that increase."

"Yield? Do you know what you are asking?"

"Not I, Priden. It is He who asks, and there is but one life-answer. Let your answer be *yes*," encouraged Deep Joy. "You can trust Son and Master Gardener."

"You're sure about this? I can just lose myself and He will find me? He will catch me? It's that simple?" Priden asked, wanting to believe it might be true.

"Yes, we can do this Priden. Son has done His part. Now it's time for our part."

"And guess what else Priden? We are to share an inheritance with Master Gardener and Son—Heaven *and* Earth," Deep Joy explained.

"Whoa, two places at once?" asked Priden disbelieving. "Those are theirs, right? So why would they share all that with us?"

"They are all about family and they embrace us as part of that family. Therefore, we share all things as one unified body. Listen, just think about it. The soaking today is a mighty one. We can really let go. Something good is bound to happen. Just breathe one more time…"

Priden swallowed and then did just that as he had this thought: *"Joint Heir."*

CHAPTER TWO

Pressing: Entrenched and Rooting

The Earth held its breath in the precious moments surrounding Priden's surrender. Not one thing could disturb the peace of this time. Priden, and many others that Master Gardener had planted, rested still and quiet in their spot of earth. Hours and hours rolled by. Breath was gone and an ultimate hush clamped down over everything. This is what it meant to be held, fastened. One would think all was over, for what could possibly be done at a time like this? There's no song, no whisper, no thought. Stillness is all that exists.

Master Gardener rose and began to walk the land. Each step marked His stamp of approval in the soil. Seedlings were submitting to new life throughout the Earth. This was a "letting go" that had cost each one something. It didn't mean that the cost was the same for everyone, but payment was always sacrificial—the most they could give. Oh, how He would bless them one by one, for now, they were becoming co-laborers with Son, Master Gardener's beloved.

The Gardener hummed His love song into the quiet. Life rustled herself and began to moan in the core of every being. The moan increased in strength, gathering energy from a source not its own. Soon, what was a moan became a persistent roar thrashing within the walls of each seedling. The Earth was drunk with the soakings and though the weight of them was severe, they could not match the expansion of the aching sound from within each new creation. In that second, the covering split and Life escaped her shell. Priden gasped for air.

"What's happening? Something has happened! I feel different. It's like there are two parts of me and an anchor holding me in place!" said Priden.

"It's a root, Priden. It's the taproot that Son told us about," cried Deep Joy.

"What do I need it for? What is it supposed to do? I never had one before," Priden declared.

"Let's ask Son. He's ahead of us. He must know," said Deep Joy. "Son…Son, are you listening?"

"Always, Deep Joy. Tell me what you wish to talk about," replied Son.

"Well, Priden and I, and, well, others too perhaps, are trying to understand what just happened to us. One minute, we were firm seeds, and now we seem to be falling apart with anchors springing forth for some unknown reason. Can You help us understand what's going on?" inquired Deep Joy.

"Yeah Son, what's going on here? This feels so weird. I'm not used to this! Can we go back to what we used to be like?" Priden pleaded.

"Priden, speak for yourself!" chuckled Deep Joy. "There's no way that I want to go back to 'the old'. New things hold such interesting promise, even adventure, but let's hear Son now. Ah, we're listening, Son," she said respectfully.

Son sighed and began, "Be not afraid. The soil is loaded with good things. Even the soakings bring nutrients, but without a root system, we'd have no way to nurse from the land. Master Gardener has cultivated the land to sustain Life. He knows where we are and what we stand in need of. By His word, all that is required has been given. Even I have been given to bring eternal things for all. Just trust that great is His wisdom."

"So this is a new and...and *permanent* life?" asked Priden.

"A new phase of life has been given Priden. There are many cycles in your existence, many turns in the road. You don't just come to a certain point and exist no more. We all must press in and journey on," explained Son.

Deep Joy sighed, obviously grateful for all that was taking place. This was going to be the adventure she had always dreamed of. Something new would be happening all the time and she got to be included. What a grand plan!

"Son," she called. "How does our root system work? Is there something special for us to do?"

"Ask and it shall be given. Seek and ye shall find. Knock and it shall be opened unto you." [Matt. 7:7] "All you need is right here for the taking. It's the root that can absorb it all. As it finds nourishment, the body is supplied, satisfied," reported Son.

"And how do You know these things, Son?" inquired Priden.

"I am the Root and the Offspring of David, and the bright Morning Star." [Rev. 22:16] "Master Gardener planted Me in the earth to show all creation the way back to Him, the Father. My life stands as an example of how these things are to come to pass," replied Son. "Trust that I am the way, the truth and the life." [Jn. 14:6]

"I want to trust You," quipped Priden. "In fact, something just tells me that I should, but it's hard to believe that You just stumbled on this information just like that. Who told You all of this? And why didn't they tell me about it?"

"I have been with the Master Gardener for forever. There are things He and I just know from Our time of being together. It is hard for you to understand this, but We knew you before you were even a seedling. We've known of you for forever," Son explained.

"Now that's fascinating! You've been around for forever and You've known of me for that same amount of time. Wow! This just gets trickier and trickier! But You see, it's just that I feel like *I've* been there for me all along!"

"Yes, but again, I've been there for you forever—even before you were in the womb of the Earth." [Jeremiah 1:5] "And Priden, you did trust Me earlier. Remember? When you stopped everything? In that instant you let go of self and allowed another to be in control. That one was Me, and you can have faith in Me even now. You see, letting go is not a one-time event. It becomes a way of life—something you do every day. What makes this simple for you is that you can cast your care upon Me, for it is I who care for you," Son responded. [1 Peter 5:7]

"Don't You expect *me* to care for *me*?" asked Priden.

"No. You are to love yourself by letting *Me* care for you. Your care will never be quite strong enough, and that is why I gladly meet this need for you. There is no shame in having Me watch over you. Once others know that I am the Saving One, they too will want, and welcome, My care and protection; for in My care, all are ultimately safe."

"Why do You offer such protection" asked Priden. "There must be some pay-off for You."

"My reward is given by My Father. Knowing that He is pleased is really payment enough. And then, there's the added bonus of knowing that the Evil One does not get to steal the Father's children, My brothers and sisters. We're family. That is the biggest joy," Son answered. "Try to rest now Priden," He added. "This is enough for you to ponder at one time."

"Yes, I suppose it is," sighed Priden.

Silence returned to the area, but with it came a fresh dose of moisture. Each one welcomed the moisture; some even sought it out before it touched them. Priden waited for the cool liquid to greet him, for he was in no hurry to chase anything. Son had given him a lot to think about. There was a plan in motion all around him. He had not developed it, but he was definitely in the midst of it. Someone beyond himself had thought of everything. The fact that he and all creation were being threatened and needed a helper; the truth that creation was afraid and needed to be taught to believe and trust that this Someone had the power to truly rescue them; and lastly, the *reality* that creation could choose to accept or reject the help—all of these things were novel ideas.

Wow, to think that everyone had a huge dose of choice to maneuver. How phenomenal! Master Gardener actually wanted the created beings to pick and choose whenever they felt like it. What kind of person gives away power like that?

Priden mused over all these things as he crouched deeper becoming more snug in his spot. The Earth began to make room for the roots of all who sought the soakings. Energy surged forth feeding them all. Sustenance was there for the taking. No performance was necessary, except to submit. That was the only requirement—submission. One only had to *allow* the exchange to happen. No attendants were there to force this transfer. They wouldn't have wanted to even if they could bring such a demand to pass. This thing called Choice was a freedom that said, 'I love you and I'm going to trust you with everything even if it means you will choose against me.' How could Son and Master Gardener give the created ones that much authority? Priden could not understand it fully, but he was beginning to see that, just possibly, he had never known what it meant to have real control, or real love, for that matter. Was he ready for true power? Could he handle deciding his own destiny? What if he chose poorly? Would he get other chances? Would he harm others? Perhaps he would hurt himself! Gosh, what would happen then?

"So many questions, right Priden?" interrupted Deep Joy.

"Whoa! You startled me Deep Joy! And, how did you know I was asking a bunch of questions just now?" asked Priden.

"Well, this is all so new for so many. It's not the easiest thing to just surrender ourselves to another. I'd say it takes some getting used to, but when you look at the benefits, I think you'll see that it's well worth the effort."

"Yeah, there are benefits already. As soon as I sense that I'm drying out, I stretch toward the moisture and, before I know it, I am infused with health," admitted Priden. "Talk about being tapped into a pipeline!"

"Yes! There's something to stretching toward good things. I've heard Son talk about that before. It sounded like Master Gardener could have dropped gifts on us, but He decided to only make them available to us. That way we could choose whether to grab them or not. Our effort would only involve reaching for them and believing them to be there," Deep Joy informed him.

"Hold it, Deep Joy," Priden whispered suddenly.

"What? I was just…"

"*Shhh*! Wait…you hear that? Sounds like somebody's coming this way! How can that be?" asked Priden.

The question hung in space against the approaching sound and all that it would bring. Priden and Deep Joy were poised and listening as the sound came closer and closer until suddenly it stopped. Both sucked in air not knowing whether to speak. Heartbeats resounded in their minds as fear tried to cling to them.

Finally, Deep Joy could take it no longer and said slowly, "Hello out there. Can you hear me?"

"What? Who me? Are you talking to me?" was the out-of-breath answer.

"Well, yes. You're new around here and we don't know your name. My name is Deep Joy, by the way, and this is Priden." Priden threw in a 'howdy' and waited again for the stranger to speak.

"Good to meet you both. I didn't know who would be on this side. I only knew I had to go after the water. It's doing so much for me, releasing me from this dark place."

Priden became excited and tried hard to lean toward the newcomer for more info. "Go on," he encouraged. "Tell us what that means."

"First of all, my name is Hunthir. It means to hunger and thirst; somehow I can't get enough food and drink so I keep scouting for more. You see, where I come from has been such a dry place, or maybe it's that I dried it out. I can't tell which came first. But anyway, once things get powdery, I move on as fast as possible. It doesn't pay to stick around too long," he explained.

"Wow, so you've ended up all the way over here in your quest," mused Deep Joy.

Priden pitched forth with, "You're not here to dry out this area, are you Hunthir? We can't have that you know!" Anxiety cloaked his words like mud.

"Well, usually my drive causes others to hunger and thirst as well. You too will see that traveling will strengthen you and cause you to break through the depths of this darkness."

"You haven't escaped Hunthir. You're down here just like us. No different, no freer, and probably no wiser," Priden accused.

"Oh, but you're wrong, Priden. I am *here* and I am *there* all at the same time. As I travel, I try to let everyone know that rooting about for real sustenance is what's needed to break through the surface of earth. The very top of you will explode in that direction giving you a new vantage point. It's like you become a new creation. The old stays below the surface, buried, but the new you pushes up and comes forth free, totally unconfined," he declared.

"Go on," Deep Joy urged ready to hear more about a new life.

"Yeah, keep going, Hunthir. This escape business is what our friend Son mentioned. We spoke with Him earlier. Maybe you know Him," Priden commented.

"Know him? Well, sure I do! He's up above. It's beautiful to watch Him in the light. I can't wait for you to see for yourselves. Anyway, just so you understand, we have nothing to lose by rooting around down here. There's everything to gain," Hunthir explained.

"What can we gain? It seems so futile to root around for who knows what."

"Well, look there," Hunthir pointed. "We're just coming to that…"

CHAPTER THREE

Leafing: Sprouted and Feeding

"Wow, there's a glow up there!" exclaimed Priden.

"Yes! This is it! Everybody push! Come on Priden. Push!" cried Hunthir.

Everyone strained with all the effort they could find. Breathing became loud as each groaned into the last push.

"My, it's getting brighter!" squealed Deep Joy. "What does this mean?"

"It means we're breaking through into His marvelous light. He dropped us from above and, with one final heave, this is where we return! My goodness it's glorious, isn't it!" Hunthir announced.

"Yes and now I can see. I mean, *really* see! Look at us! We never had this form before! We're even a different color!" Priden said marveling at himself and the others. *If only my buddies could see me like this. Wouldn't they be surprised*, Priden thought, but he dared not brag that idea aloud.

"Yes. What is this form called Hunthir?" asked Deep Joy.

"I'm not sure, but the One over there seems to have many of them. Let's ask Him. I believe He might be the One I've been seeking," Hunthir replied.

They all looked in the direction of the One who had many of the forms they were now beginning to have. Deep Joy called out, "Oh excuse me. You there! What's Your Name and what form is this you bear in such abundance?"

"Hi Deep Joy. It is Me, Son. Remember?"

"Son! Why I'd know that voice anywhere! Yes! Hey everyone, this is our own Son! He came down below to show us the way to freedom," Deep Joy laughed gleefully as her new form unfolded a bit more from all the chuckling.

"Son," Priden called. "Oh Son, You did promise a way out! I never expected it would be like this. If you had explained it, I'm sure I never would have understood such wonder. I hate to admit it, but You were, well, You were right. Letting go was the only way out. My plan would have never effected this. Compared with Your idea, my way wasn't even a pebble in a mountain."

"Don't be hard on yourself, Priden. You never knew Me before, so you were relying on the only one you did know— yourself. But we know each other now and things can be so very different. And speaking of difference, your new form is called *leaves*. They soak up the light of the Master Gardener, and by this we are sustained even more. It is exceedingly good to be full of His light. It makes us like Him."

Hunthir, Deep Joy, and Priden looked at each other musing over the meaning of all this newness. As they sighed, their leaves unfurled all the more and light filled them with warmth and peace. Their leaves became firm and rested on the wind, outstretched and surrendered. A gentle breeze nudged at them, but they held their place all the more.

"How grand this is," chirped Deep Joy.

Priden interrupted her with a complaining look, but Deep Joy continued.

"No, really! *This* is grand! We have come out of the depths to step into a realm of living like we've never known. We have left darkness and stepped into His glorious light!" [1 Peter 2:9] "Don't you see? This was planned all along by Master Gardener! All we had to do was believe He would provide—not that we could make anything happen, but that *He* would make every provision! How special we must be to Him," she beamed.

"Special? It seems to me that Master Gardener could have told us in advance what we could expect. I could have saved myself some planning time. Does He know how I agonized over what to do? I was the one who was really worried about us all! Why I…"

"I hate to interrupt you friend," said Hunthir, "but sometimes it's not about us and what we think. His thoughts have always been higher than our thoughts. And His ways are certainly higher than even our most expanded ways." [Isa. 55:9] "He knows the end from the very beginning and has certainly read, categorized, and filed all of what's in the middle!" [Isa. 46:10] "I don't think we can beat Him at what He does, because He does it so well. We're talking *perfection* here. Every detail covered. No leftovers waiting for attention. He took care of everything! How can you top that?"

Priden chimed in, "Well, I just think He could have spared me all that effort."

"Priden," Hunthir cried, "He *did* save us and that's worth something. Actually, it's worth everything! We could be rotting in the depths of darkness, cold and soaked to the rotten core of our being. But He chose to give us a way out, to shape us anew and release us to be all that He knows we can be. I can't believe you don't see this!"

Priden shrugged, wanting the conversation to be over. He was sure that Hunthir did not know what he was talking about. How could he make Hunthir understand the importance of time, which was definitely not a thing to be abused. Surely, everyone needed to know that there are times when things simply must be pointed out. In fact, it couldn't hurt to always make this a practice. Why should merely mentioning a thing be a crime? Priden pondered over these ideas not knowing what to say in this awkward moment. Just as musing became difficult, a warm breeze rustled everyone's leaves. Priden shook with the rest wishing that for just a minute he could feel enough control to be comfortable again.

CHAPTER FOUR

Growing: Changed and Moving

Gentle breezes blew. Winds whipped. Rains came and Priden and his friends thrived. No one complained and life took on effortless motion. Weeks curled around them and vanished. Just when everyone was at total peace, the sun began to bear down on their leaves. Each planting had many leaves due to the rich conditions they had all been blessed to receive. How could they not be prosperous in a time like that? However, great times can be fleeting, temporary, and then what?

The first few days of heat were simply annoying. The plantings assumed rain would return any hour, but rain did not pay them a visit. No cloud of hers entered any part of the vast sky above. The heat had an open highway to their leaves, stems, and stalks. What could be done to stop this onslaught?

Another day passed. As the sun crept into the sky, all the plantings braced themselves. The bottom leaves moved into the shade of the upper leaves. However, by noon, the top leaves were limp and unable to shade anyone. The lowest leaves could still feel moisture from the root, but they could not give shade to anyone.

The stalks straightened themselves as much as possible and passed any droplet of moisture they could to their neighboring stems who in turn gave a portion to their thirsty leaves. Everyone worked to supply every part of the planting, but all would be lost if the Sun did not relent soon. [Eph. 4:16] How long could they last this way?

Another day came and went. Priden was delirious with misery. He began to say things like, "Was this Master Gardener's big Plan? Why, we'd be better off back in the darkness! The heat couldn't bake us then!"

Deep Joy tried to reassure Priden that, even now, some sort of relief would be there for them. All they had to do was wait expectantly.

Well, Priden did not want to hear all that positive stuff from Deep Joy and he hoped this comment would not get Meek or Hunthir to start in on him again. His hopes were not strong enough though because, sure enough, Hunthir stirred himself enough to make a few comments of his own.

"Priden," he called, "This is that place of hungering and thirsting after righteousness." [Mt. 5:6] "We long with all that is in us right now to reach the One who can quench our thirst forever. There is no other thought or desire on our minds right now. We only want Him who can save us."

Priden quipped back, "Well, if it's longing that works, then your longing alone, Hunthir, should have saved us already!"

"Perhaps He wants our corporate longing this time Priden. Can you commit to a joint longing?" asked Hunthir.

"Well, I don't know about the hungering part. I do feel some of that, but I really do thirst now. I'm so thirsty for real water. If He could just give us a bit of pond water. Look, we're about to pass out!" Priden responded.

"We shall reap a harvest in due season, if we faint not," Deep Joy managed to say. [Gal. 6:9] She was feeling a little woozy now too, but she knew Master Gardener would provide a way of escape. She believed, simply and profoundly believed.

Just then, Son began the softest prayer:

"To the One who knows all things,
I ask for strength in this hour,
Give us all that we stand in need of,
For we are ready to receive it,
And I thank You for always hearing Me."

When Son paused, the others said, "Amen," and before the word finished ringing in the air, a rain drop touched Priden's most withered leaf, scaring him nearly to death.

"Where did that come from?" he yelled as he looked up. No one had noticed that a cloud was hovering over them! Wow, they not only had shade, but this mighty cloud held the promise of hours of rain! And oh, how it did rain! Water ran and danced at the base of their stalks, seeping its way into the ground to encourage the roots to drink and drink some more.

Deep Joy laughed with joy. Never had she been so full of delight. Meek gladly sighed his appreciation for this wonderful gift and Hunthir added big tears to the bouncing droplets. He too was overcome with gratitude. Once again, his prayers and those of others had been answered.

Priden just looked in amazement. Water was falling every-where. He noticed that he could still hear Son's prayer spinning around in his head. *Could it all be connected,* he wondered, *the asking and receiving? This is something I will have to witness again in order to be firmly convinced, but right now, I admit that I am enjoying this dousing. Woohoo!!! The rain came! I'm not sure how, but it came. Someone else can worry with how it came…or is that my worry?*

Something is definitely wrong here. I'm not so sure of things. In fact, I'm not sure of anything anymore. I see how Deep Joy has a steady, sturdy confidence, but not in herself. And that guy Meek, though different, he is just as steady. Now Hunthir, he's the zaniest of them all, yet he is on one path too—no wavering, no wandering. How did they get like that?

And then there is Son. He's the hardest to figure out. He's simple, yet complicated all at the same time. He knows everything! It's like He's been here before, done all of this, knows what's coming and just lives the moment—no worries, no cares. No questions even! He's all answers! There is no one like Him, but everyone is trying to be like Him. That's probably why we all fell silent when He prayed. I still hear it—the "needing" and "receiving" part. There must be something to that. I guess He'll show me. I almost want to ask Him about it right now. Who knows, He probably even realizes that I'm thinking this. It's hard to believe that I'm mulling over this stuff. Guess things have changed some. Perhaps I'm different or maybe becoming different. Priden chuckles, then sighs, *My, my! Change is slow, but it does come. And it's not so bad when it shows up.*

Little miracles happen all over the land as withering leaves plump up in response to the timeliest rain they've ever known.

CHAPTER FIVE

Standing: Stretched and Climbing

Calm returned to the land and the plantings settled into daily routines. Comfort became their friend and all knew Peace to be their neighbor. No one suspected that such tranquility was about to be snapped in two—no one, that is, except Hunthir.

Days went by and Hunthir had become increasingly uncomfortable in his spirit. He could not explain what it was. All *seemed* fine. Everyone was growing bit by bit. Each hour came with the right amount of light and nutrition; even the air was plant-friendly, trading secret ingredients for the health of all, but something was just not right.

Son was in deeper thought than usual. Not a word had come from him in days, only sighs and groaning. Was He communing with someone? Hunthir could not stand it anymore and he cleared his throat to speak. "Son, I haven't wanted to say anything, but something is happening or about to happen, isn't it?"

Son spoke comfortingly, "We must be still and know that the Master Gardener is who He says He is. We must not let our hearts be troubled or even let them be afraid." [John 14:27] "We are taken care of by His own awesome hand."

"But haven't You felt like something is on the way? I can't spell it all out, but I know something is about to happen. I just sense it, Son."

"Then be prayerful. Do not grow weary in well doing for you will reap a harvest if you faint not," replied Son. [Gal. 6:9]

"I try not to worry. It's just that *not knowing* can sometimes make me nervous. Many times I've been caught off guard by awful things. I never saw them coming and when they hit, it was hard to prepare to defeat them."

"But you're here, aren't you?"

"Yes."

"So that means you made it past those awful times," Son triumphed, "you and Master Gardener together. So now you know."

"Know what, Son," asked Hunthir.

"Who to trust. Trust in *Him* with all your heart and lean not on your own understanding. Acknowledge His ways and He will direct your path." [Prov. 3: 5-6]

Hunthir thought about this and then uttered, "Is it really that simple, Son?"

"Yes, this yoke is easy Hunthir. Master Gardener doesn't want you to carry any heavy burdens. Your hunger for truth is admirable, but even this must be balanced. Too much or too little is not helpful or needful. Rest is found in the middle. Let Him take you there," encouraged Son.

"How can I do this?" cried Hunthir.

"Believe and have faith that each day your steps will be directed by Him. Just let go and let Him do the rest," said Son.

"Son, letting go is rather passive isn't it? Aren't we supposed to have some works to show our faith level?"

"You're to have faith so that it can make your works effective. It is faith that says, 'Because I trust Him, I will act when he says act and I'll be inactive when he says to wait.' That's trust-level faith," Son explained.

"Then I will rest as you say Son. It's not important that I'm ready for what's coming, rather it's *everything* that He's prepared for it." Hunthir paused and then added, "Oh by the way Son, how do You know so much about Master Gardener?"

"We're close relatives," Son returned.

"Wow, You're an excellent role model, Son. Master Gardener must be proud."

Son simply smiled.

Days passed and the plantings grew. The heat spell did not come back to dissolve the great weather. Everyone was glad. Occasionally, Hunthir thought about his talk with Son. Grabbing all of the meaning was not easy, but Son had the most assured way of answering Hunthir's questions. Hunthir wondered what Priden would think of all these things. Priden had resisted much of what was required here, whereas Hunthir both studied and surveyed what was happening. Yet each one was flourishing nicely despite their varied dispositions.

Late one night, when only half the moon shone upon them, little feet began to move in the distance. It was a quiet walk at first and then something took flight batting the air with the sheerest of wings. The plantings breathed and slept, not suspecting that visitors were well on the way, uninvited but determined to introduce themselves.

The first guest landed on snoring Priden. With an extra snort, he shook himself and resumed the most careful snooze he could manage. However, in a moment he was bumped again. Waving his leaves a bit, he dislodged the intruder and settled back into a moderate snore.

Then just when night was perfectly still, every possible planting dream was ripped apart by the scream of Deep Joy. It knifed through the air, sounding an alarm that defied being ignored. Even the winged creatures paused in their flight.

"What's this?" Deep Joy exclaimed. "There are little green things all over me and I can't get them off!"

"Me either!" yelled Priden.

"What's going on?" quipped Hunthir.

As the night collected itself, the plantings were able to see tiny life things crawling on them. The creatures' feet tickled the stalks of the plantings and eased upward bit by bit. They had six legs, red eyes, and spiky lime-green bodies that were nearly transparent. Grayish wings continued to fan the air as they looked for places to land.

"We need Wind to shift. Maybe that would send them back," offered Priden. "Let's ask. Oh Wind, can you please change course? Look what has flown in! These critters are disturbing our rest. How are we supposed to grow like this?"

"I know how you feel Priden. It's certainly not fair that they blew in unannounced and certainly uninvited. Once they stick to you though, there's not a lot that I can do. If they become airborne, I can lift them away, but they seem quite content on your limbs," Wind responded.

Priden was fuming. "Deep Joy, are you okay? Wherever did you get that ice-melting scream?"

"Oh Priden, I am not usually like this, but I was aroused from a happy sleep by the most terrible sting under one of my leafings. I didn't know what was going on and I hollered at the pain from the sting."

"One of your leaves was pinched?" Priden asked.

"Yes. Weren't some of yours?"

"No, or at least not…"

"Owwww!"

Priden frantically looked about. "Who was that," he demanded. "Who just screamed?"

"Me! Hunthir! These creatures are feeding on our leafings! Oh, make them stop!"

Others began to feel the stinging and gnawing. You could almost hear the chorus of sucking. The leafings were in for a fight, but what weapon could they use? Hunthir thought back to his conversation with Son. Somehow this must be the moment to let go and let Master Gardener take over. If only they could trust in Him completely. Hunthir knew he must try, so he held himself perfectly still and waited. Just at that moment, a thought entered Hunthir's mind, *stretch*. What could that mean—*stretch*? Again it came, *stretch*. Hunthir tried the word on for size and spoke it into the approaching dawn, "S-t-r-e-t-c-h!"

He breathed deeply and moved a smidgin' higher. Amazingly, a critter lost its grip and fell off! When it hit the ground, its wings were smashed and it died from other injuries! Hunthir, not wanting to jump to any quick conclusion, tried this experiment again. This time, three critters fell to their deaths.

"Wow! That's it! Hey, everybody! Stretch! The critters can't keep their grip if you stretch upward! When they hit the ground, their wings shatter and they die! Come on everybody, you can do it! Stretch! Look up and stretch," yelled Hunthir.

Not having anything to lose, everyone followed Hunthir's example. Critters were hitting the dust by the hundreds. The plan worked. The Sun began to bring the day, making it easier for the stretching to continue. Critters were dropping everywhere. Some lived longer than others, but once the Sun was fully up, it was clear they could not bear the heat.

Everyone celebrated how well this simple strategy had defeated their enemy. The stretching caused them all to climb to a height they had not known before and it was beautiful to see how tall they could stand. Wind applauded causing them to bow in unison. What a victory!

Deep Joy could hardly contain how thrilling this was to her. She had to know how Hunthir figured out what to do. "Hunthir, have you had this experience before? Where did you learn this secret?"

"The secret wasn't stretching, Deep Joy. The secret was letting go and trusting that Master Gardener would take care of us. He's the One who knew about stretching."

"Master Gardener?" yelled Priden. "He never showed up. He hasn't been around in a long time. We've been left here to fend for ourselves!" Priden crossed two leaves in protest.

"No, you're wrong Priden," Hunthir said. "I heard a thought that I truly believe was given to me by Him. He saw, or knew, that I was covered with the enemy. I stood still, waiting and listening. That's when I heard Him. He commanded me to stretch. When I questioned it just to be double-sure, He repeated it and not once, but twice! What did I have to lose? I decided to exercise my faith, and so I stretched! That's when I saw the first critter fall off and die. I knew then that I had to bring you all in on His strategy. But He wasn't done even then. The Sun beat this enemy also. They can't thrive in the light of day. Light brings heat with it and that's why they showed up at night. It was cool and dark then, but rest assured that Master Gardener knew our dilemma and the Sun came up on time with no clouds to hide Him. This, I believe, came from Master Gardener."

"You want to believe real bad, Hunthir," Priden said sarcastically.

"No, I *do* believe, Priden, and it's *believing* that makes us whole. Somewhere along the way, I heard someone say that believing is called faith!"

"Faith?" repeated Priden.

"Yes, faith," replied Hunthir. "And it's been said that the best faith is the kind that goes on believing when it makes no natural sense to do so. You just make up your mind to believe no matter what, and at all costs, simply believe. Then you'll see powerful things working from the shoulders of that kind of faith. Enemies don't know what to do with it, but the person with it knows to simply keep using it."

Deep Joy had been listening and waiting for a chance to enter this conversation. Finally, when she could stand it no longer, she cleared her throat and the others looked her way. "Well, I kind of like how we believed enough to flow in unison.

Those critters made their move *together*, but so did we. Once our 'weapon' was drawn, we all wielded it together. There's something to be said for that, don't you think?"

"You're right," Hunthir replied. "And even though we may not sound like we're in agreement now, we certainly moved as one stretching machine then! That was power and it was exactly that power that pushed the enemy right out of here!"

Suddenly, Son commented, "The Spirit of One Accord always stands more powerful than a divided front."

"Yes," said Deep Joy. "That's it. We were moving with One Accord. All were in agreement, no division. How could we not be successful?"

"Hmmm," said Priden. "We just got lucky, wouldn't you say? I mean, Hunthir just *happened* to figure out that stretching was going to help us, didn't he?"

"No Priden. Don't you get it? I was clueless about *what* to do and had to be *told* what to try. The first step in all of this was to admit that I did not have the answers. That's the first thing that has to happen at a time like this—admission of need. At some point, you've got to introduce yourself to the fact that you do not have absolute control. In fact, most of the time, none of us has any control whatsoever!"

"Now, that can't be! We've got to be responsible for some things, don't we?" Priden nearly bragged.

Deep Joy piped in, "I think what we're responsible for is knowing who's *really* responsible. I know that I need that someone to be somebody other than me, somebody bigger—truly bigger in thoughts, plans and deeds."

"And who fits that mighty bill?" Priden inquired.

"Why, Master Gardener...and Son. You know, I hear they're close relatives," Hunthir added.

"Here we go. Master Gardener, Master Gardener! Our hero once again! Look everyone, if it weren't for Him, we wouldn't be in this place at all! Don't you see that yet?" Priden begged.

"Priden, I'd hate to think where we would be if it hadn't been for Master Gardener," said Deep Joy. "You may not value what we have, but from my vantage point, we've done well here. We've learned a lot and have flourished despite adversity. You'll understand in time, dear friend. I know you will," Deep Joy added.

"Time?" he mumbled. "That's the part that gets in the way. Some things just take *too much time*!"

"Well, in the grand scheme of things, time as we know it, is long; but as Master Gardener knows it, there are no markers. *We* place marks all over time. Time for this, time for that. Time to be and time not to be. Master Gardener does not start and end time. He made it from the standpoint that it has always been and always will be, uninterrupted. He calls it *eternity* which by another term means forever. We get to *be* forever. So, in the meantime, what you are experiencing here is only a blimp on the screen of forever. Our *now* is happening so fast in the face of eternity, we can scarce keep up with it."

"Now that brings me to Step Two, Priden," adds Hunthir. "When you think about the vastness of eternity, it has to be evident that somehow, it is someone else who has all of the real answers. I'm serious, Priden. It's true that someone else is—uh—now hold on to your seat for this," and he whispers, "Someone else is...in...control."

Silence crowded around those last words. No one moved. Could it all come down to this issue—control? *What's a little control anyway*, Priden wondered. *It's just taking charge, running things, knowing about everything. Why, there are no surprises when one has absolute control. No one can sneak in a maneuver. How about that? And the 'feel good' is oh so sweet. So what can be wrong about being in control?* All of these thoughts danced in Priden's mind.

"I know what you're thinking, Priden, and yes, *control* is a fine thing, that is, if you are the one who possesses it. But if you're not, then you must look to the One who does own it. Outside of that, there's no hope, no safety," Hunthir warned.

"Well, I've always been made to feel responsible for everything—responsible for being right, and definitely responsible for when I'm wrong. Folks can lay some heavy guilt on you when you're wrong, and those times are not easily forgotten. I can remember a time when I did something nice for someone. Did they see the kindness, the motive? No! They saw a safety risk in the midst of the kind act and had me punished for running what they felt was a risk. It's been hard to forget. They made it clear how 'responsible' I was. So now, I try my hardest to take better care of my 'responsibilities,'" Priden added with much emphasis.

Hunthir chimed in again, "But that's a lot of work for you, Priden. Master Gardener wants you to be relieved of all that. He's suffered some things so you won't have to suffer so. Remember, 'His yoke is easy and his burden is light.' You're to have the easy, light way. Why be under such a heavy weight of total responsibility when there's One who has come to remove that weight?" [Matt. 11:30]

"Well, if I'm weighted down, he should just take some of the load then."

"Have you tried offering Him the load? You have to be willing to release the load to Him Priden, and then step back so you won't be tempted to pick it up again."

"Yeah, Priden," Deep Joy added, "step away from the load and watch Him take it completely because that's really the Third Step in all of this. We must each recognize that the One in control is Master Gardener. It's not enough to say, 'I'm not in control' and 'Someone else is.' We must see that the 'Someone else' is Him who created us all. He's been here from the very beginning, and He will be here for all eternity."

"Gosh, that sounds great, but it's not that easy. I guess sometimes I feel myself wavering and maybe a part of me wants to relax and let someone else do *it*, but letting go of it all is tricky. I bet I've sort of let go, and then just picked everything right back up again," Priden confessed. "I just knew something would go wrong and maybe it would be wrong enough that I would be blamed. There's something about *blame* that I can't stand, you know?"

"Well, when we're blamed, we take it to mean there's something bad about ourselves. Oftentimes, something just goes wrong period, and it has nothing to do with whether we are good or bad," said Deep Joy.

"Right," Priden said sarcastically.

"Aww, Priden, just know that He works all things together for our good," answered Deep Joy. [Rom. 8:28] "That means the good and the bad count for something. We learn something from each life event. Nothing is wasted."

"Sometimes I just don't care to be bothered with finding out whether it was *me* or *it* that went wrong, so I take over to make sure *everything* is right the first time," Priden responded.

Deep Joy waited and then said softly but deliberately, "Fear is a vicious animal, Priden."

"Fear! Who said anything about fear? I'm not afraid of anything if that's what you're trying to say," Priden added with a sloppy laugh.

Deep Joy looked directly at Priden and said, "Priden, listen to me. Fear will bark and growl about how you will pay if *this* or *that* isn't perfect. Mr. Fear will lick his lips and tell you that you're no good if *this* doesn't get done a certain way or if *that* isn't accomplished by a certain time. Next, he'll pounce all over your best efforts and cause you to believe that, yet again, you weren't the best. Finally, when he has you in a tight corner, he doesn't even need to threaten to bite you. He knows you're afraid enough to bite yourself! He can step back with a mission-accomplished grin and fold his arms across his mean ole chest while you beat yourself into the ground trying to control everything for the sake of measuring up."

Priden blinked and swallowed hard, looking desperately for a rebuttal, but Deep Joy continued.

"Priden, you are of more value than that. Master Gardener declares this to be so. You are the head and not the tail." [Deut. 28:13] "Nothing is to stand in your way. Corners are not to be your residence. You are to operate from much finer headquarters knowing who the One in command is. I therefore announce today that fear can no longer taunt you, Priden. You are released from his grip as of this moment. He has no claim to you and you are free to be you! Are you in agreement with this decree?"

"Three steps? Just three steps?" asked Priden.

"Yes. Only three," answered Deep Joy.

"Then I guess I agree," he said, and, for the first time, Priden wept for joy.

CHAPTER SIX

Flowering: Budded and Blooming

As the Sun began to smile brightly on the new day, there seemed to be an air of expectation all around the plantings. The ground was warmer, the river brighter. Creatures hummed in near unison as time moved toward something new. No one knew what that something might be, but it was clear that something was imminent. All felt that the event would be special. No hindrances or obstacles stood in the way, and how could they? An atmosphere of "one accord" had established itself overnight. Priden had given himself over to a willingness to see Master Gardener as the One in charge of all things and with that…

…the first bud formed on each planting. A bead of budding faith came from within announcing its connection with Sun. Oh how it nearly overwhelmed Priden to see this measure of change. And to have it happen so quickly was staggering! Priden marveled that he was included in this miracle. In fact, he couldn't help but wonder how he could deserve such an honor given his past attitude.

Later, he began wondering why he had taken so long to see and hear the truth. "It really is true that we can *let go* and let Master Gardener carry us," he announced to anyone who would listen. "How He has chosen to favor me though is still a bit mysterious," he murmured.

Deep Joy pranced into Priden's musing, "Before you run down the road of regrets and why-didn't-Is, you must know that all of this is for nothing if you're going to blame yourself. You're to feel no shame now. That's been covered by the One who loves you best. He sacrificed all for you by sending His Son to die for you. Then He raises Him from the dead as an example of how we too can be raised. It's an 'O happy day' moment, Priden, not an 'O woe is me' time!"

A moment later she asked, "Have you seen Son lately?"

"Well, no, I haven't."

"Take a look over there," she said bowing slightly in the direction that lead to Son.

Priden peered past many plantings until his eyes came to rest on some thick bars. "I see a rod or two over there past the plantings, Deep Joy. Is that the spot?" asked Priden.

"Look up silly! Look way up!" Deep Joy giggled.

"What?" Priden asked as he leaned back to look up as high as possible. "Whoa, what happened? Son is so tall and what are those round things? He must have a ton of them! They look so heavy, but my, they are bright...and...and they're way up there!" exclaimed Priden.

"He has reached new heights Priden! This is the fullness of His Glory—the Son of Master Gardener. Look how majestic He is. Such splendor! They say that some king by the name of Solomon was never robed like this!" [Matt. 6: 28-29] "Beautiful, huh?" Her eyes twinkled with glee. "And the best is that we're heading that way ourselves. That's the plan for us who believe in who He is and what He does. He is the Master come to save us from destruction. And you know, Priden, there have been plenty of attempts to destroy us."

"Well, yeah, that is so. Wow, we are about to be just like Him then! I get to stop being me and can transfer who I am to who He is? Is that how it goes?" asked Priden.

"Kind of. Actually, He is filling you with who *He* is. This way, there's a *new and improved you* created, and in that sense, the old is done away with and a totally new being comes forth. Your thoughts, your vision, even your ways become more like His. You're in sync, in unity, and anything is possible in that position."

Priden looked up again. "Wow. I hope I'm ready." With those words, it began to rain from clouds no one had even noticed before. Son was presenting so much light all around that it was hard to see any cloudiness at all, but the rain was needed. The ground swallowed it and everywhere the leaves and new buds licked at the falling moisture tasting goodness until satisfied.

Days later, what can only be described as "perking" began to happen. Perk here. Perk there. Perk, Perk, Perk. Budding things were opening. The former community of green was exploding with bright, cheerful color. Dazzling yellows, oranges, and lavenders fanned the air in high fashion. Everyone was astounded at the variety. No two were exactly the same. They varied in size and intensity of hue. Some were half the size of others. Then there were some that wore soft hues while others were blindingly rich in hue. So interesting was their new adornment that each spent lots of time getting reacquainted with their new neighbors. No parade could out-strut the pageantry displayed here.

Priden released a reluctant smile. Of all the surprises, who would have thought something this spectacular could happen. This moment was worth all the inconvenience he had ever suffered. All the soakings were merely a blur; and how could those flying critters have ever been a problem?

For the first time, Priden didn't want to disappoint Deep Joy and he said, "Deep Joy, I like what I see."

"Yeah, it is rather special isn't it Priden?" she replied. "I'm so happy to hear you are pleased."

"Yeah. We've been through a lot, but it seems to have been worth it."

They both smiled as time churned on.

Sunny.

Cloudy.

Rainy.

Sunny.

Sunny again.

Deep Joy wanted to resume her conversation with Priden. Somehow she could detect a change happening in him, and she wanted to give him as much support as she could. Later that day, she asked, "Priden, do you know what our new form is called?"

"No. I haven't heard anyone say," Priden returned.

"Well, they tell me that the *perkings* produced what's known as flowers. That means that our buds have just popped right into flowers."

"What's the flower for? What do we do with it?" he inquired.

"I'm not quite sure. Right now, it's enough to just look at each one, don't you think?"

"They are right nice to look at, but there has to be some purpose for them. Usefulness has its place doesn't it, Deep Joy? Look how long it took us to get to this flower stage. There has to be more though," Priden predicted.

"There probably is more, but in this moment, I'm content to just soak up the beauty that surrounds us. Whatever is next will come. It always does. That's the ebb and flow of life. In the meantime, let's enjoy this moment," she encouraged Priden.

"I'll try," Priden agreed. Then he added, "But I sure hope this doesn't take long."

Deep Joy chuckled silently.

Priden looked around some more. Surely all of these flowers and colors had names. Someone had to have thought of calling them something. Priden thought about names he would give if he could. *That many-petaled one would be called a "daisy," and the one with the thicker petals which seem to blister open would be a "rose." Then there's that one with lots of tiny, tiny flowers—that ought to be named "hyacinth."* Priden started to have fun coming up with fake names for these beauties. He wondered what Deep Joy would think of his little game.

"Hey Deep Joy! Wanna hear something funny?" he asked.

"What is it, Priden? I love funny things, they keep me laughing," she replied.

"I've been playing a guessing game as to what the plants could be called. I thought about how they might be identified as something more. New names, so to speak."

Deep Joy's eyes filled with such pleasure. "I think you are on to something, Priden. I heard once upon a time that we could name some things in a garden. This must be that kind of time! What have you come up with so far? I bet you are good at this!"

"Well, I *might* have a handle on it. Here's what I thought. See that medium-sized flower over there with the yellow, furry center trimmed with white spokes. I think that one should be named 'Daisy.' What do you think?" he asked.

"Well, why not? It's a good name," she answered. "We can name everyone and check with them to see if they like the names. Maybe we can even change the names after a while. You know, a new name for every season of time!"

"Okay Deep Joy, that might be taking it a little too far. Just as we are getting used to calling each other one thing, it would be confusing to have to learn the new name for everyone all at once or in staggered time. I think one name will do. Just keep it simple," begged Priden.

"Okay, Priden. I guess you're right for now. Daisy would be called *Daisy* and then *Fancy* all at once until it was clear she had switched to *Fancy*! Confusing for sure! Okay, they will have one name for now because, still, the day is coming when Master Gardener will give each of us a new name for all eternity." [Rev. 2: 17] "Just one name will be given, but for now, this means we need to carefully select the names."

"Yeah, we can be creative but certainly we will need to give the names some thought," agreed Priden.

They spent the rest of the day carefully naming every plant in the garden. By nightfall, an impressive list of all their names existed. Each was known by a Kingdom name, an Order name, a Family name of course, Tribe name, and Genus name. Each species was accounted for and had such merit. No parade stood finer.

CHAPTER SEVEN

Bowing: Curved and Bending

The days have brought their ration of nourishment and the little flowers have responded in unison. No longer are they small and frail. In fact, some have quadrupled in size, weighing the stalks down quite a bit to Priden's expressed dismay.

Moaning first, he manages to say to Hunthir, "Just when I thought things were going so well, here comes the glitch. I *knew* this was too good to be even a little bit true! Tell me why there is always a glitch to everything!"

Hunthir looks surprised. "What do you mean, Priden? We're fine. What could possibly be wrong?"

"Don't you see how big we are?" Priden asked just a touch perturbed.

"Well, yes, some of us have gotten quite large. There's more beauty to behold that way, don't you think?" Hunthir observed.

"And *more* is heavy Hunthir! Loaded down! We're all pushed over from the weight!" squawked Priden.

"We're not pushed over, Priden. Nothing is bearing down on us. Do you see anything pushed against me, Priden?"

Silence.

"Do you?" Hunthir pressed.

"No, but you're all bent just the same!" Priden chimed in.

"Well, Priden, you probably don't want to hear this, but I pray it will help nonetheless."

"What, Hunthir? Go ahead. Just spit it out."

Hunthir was growing uneasy. He so wished that Priden would just follow the course of things. Why couldn't he see that resisting everything was a miserable stance? Why hadn't he figured out that looking for the *good* gave the promise of so much happiness?

Not knowing how to begin, Hunthir looked to Son and noticed He was listening. When Son smiled, Hunthir managed to say to Priden, "Let's ask Son what He thinks. He'll know what's really going on. I love His word concerning things."

"Okay, okay." Priden swayed and then said in a loud voice, "Son. Hi. It's me—Priden. I have a question for You."

"Go ahead, Priden. What do you wish to know?" returned Son.

"Well, I see You've gotten fairly tall and even some of *us* are reaching new heights too, though not quite as high as You yet. Anyway, why is it that we're all pushed over? Everyone that has a flower has a curved back. Why is that?"

Instantly, gentle words flowed down from Son. All Priden had to do was catch them. "Priden, it's easier to simply bow."

"Bow? Did you say 'bow'?" Priden asked.

Though Son did not repeat Himself, 'bow' seemed to echo in Priden's being.

Bowww...bowwwww...

Son resumed, "This is an easy yoke and a light burden Priden. All of your being, your very existence comes down to simply bowing."

"That sounds like we're to do this on purpose, Son."

"You may do all things as you wish. There are benefits to certain actions and consequences to others, but you always have choice and therefore, liberty," Son informed him.

"I'm not sure I'm ready."

"Priden, speak to the fear and tell it to be gone," advised Son.

"What fear? Who said anything about being afraid? I'm not afraid Son. No, not me. I am not afraid," exclaimed Priden.

"Are you sure about that my friend? What will the others say once they see you totally bent?"

"I don't know what they'll think. It probably won't look pretty to be crooked though."

"And what if you can't resume your former position ever again?"

"Ugh! I did wonder about that! Would it really mean that I can't go back to the old me? Wait, why am I asking that? I'm not worried about the old me. At least I don't think I am. I know how to keep the same me...I think."

"Well, if we are honest, we do consider our former selves, especially once we see how vastly different we are becoming. It is a little startling for some, but it is a beautiful change and one that is always welcomed in the end," said Son.

"Well, maybe I have thought of it a little. It sounds like I must lose something in order to gain something. That's the part that is unsettling. Does anyone really want to put off the old in order to gain the new? That's like admitting there is something wrong with the old self. Why must that be the case? There's nothing wrong with me. I'm telling You that right now."

"Priden, it is not about being wrong. It's about becoming a *better* you. Master Gardener began a *good* work in you and He will be faithful to complete it." [Phil. 1: 6] "He's gently adding new things to the *good you* as you submit more to His plan. I'm a testament of how this occurs. Haven't you seen the change in Me? I started as a seedling too. I was left to travel this soil and to learn to stand in the midst of life's celebrations and challenges."

"Where's the calm in that, Son?" quipped Priden.

"It's in knowing Who to lean upon. I chose to lean upon Master Gardener for everything, no matter what happened. He has been My strength and support through everything. Would you like for Me to ask Him to help you Priden?" asked Son.

"Will He listen to you for me? Hey, does He even remember that I'm here?"

"Sure He does! He asks Me about you every day!"

"Every day?" Priden asks incredulously. "Why would He ask *You* about me?"

"He asks Me because I am His Son."

"What! He's Your Father?" Priden could not believe this! Son's Dad had actually been the one to release Priden into this place of no return! How could they have kept this such a secret!

"I know what you're thinking Priden. How could My Father send you here and not tell you that I am His child?

Well, guess what, Priden? He sent Me here too. As you believe in Me, He will be your Father too! This will make us brothers and we will share a vast kingdom that is to come! You see, there is so much more that is being prepared for us all!"

Priden breathed shock in and out, in again and really out again! How could this be?

Wasn't it enough to have gone through the hazards of the dark and the perils of the air? But now here he was with a being that was all-knowing and bowing to Master Gardener who truly had ultimate power and authority. Wow! The two of them actually shared all of this and were poised to rescue him?

"It's okay, Priden. It really is fine. I care about you, Priden. I pray you will decide well. Perhaps seeing more will help."

"Perhaps so. May I see these things now?" Priden asked.

"In time. In time," repeated Son.

Hours and days began to pass in regulation time. Each notch marched along unnoticed until one day something new came into being. Something quite wonderful had been happening for a while evidently, but was so gradual that it had no identity until this moment. Priden's leaves were leaning! Perhaps he would want to "un-lean" them, but it was certain that they were indeed reaching out. The reaching was in one direction, towards Son. Light shined on each leaf as if noticing each one for what it was—important and precious.

Just then Priden woke up. "Awww, time to stretch!" Priden began to move, but he could tell this was no normal stretch.

Hmph, what's wrong now, he wondered. *I don't seem to be able to move widely. I am caught on something.* Priden looked around to see others curved in one direction. Then he knew this must be the posture that he had fully assumed. How strange to be so thoroughly bent! Just a few days ago, everyone was moving upward. There was no crook in the stalks, no irregularity. *Maybe this is temporary! I sure hope so*, Priden mused.

Then his leaves lifted yet more. It was a time of feeling ready for something but he was not quite sure what that would be. Everyone looked poised for something. Expectancy hung in the air. Days moved in and out. Everyone continued ready.

Then the "complete moment" was upon them all. Somehow, the roots were fully entrenched. The stems were at total capacity. All leaves had fully expanded their arms. The flowers had formed their faces of joy, and though beautiful to behold, bowed in awe of the One who helped them all, the One who loved them all—Son. No one wanted to do anything else, just bow and keep on bowing. Bow, sway some, but bow.

CHAPTER EIGHT

Producing: Filled and Giving

With heavy heads bowed, the flowers began receiving guests. Friendly bees visited many of the flowers and began to share the goodness of the flowers with others. All was ripe and ready for supporting life to come. Priden did not understand how the flowers did not seem to mind this goodness being taken. He chimed in to all the buzzing, "Why have you come to steal what is ours? Did you ask for permission? Where are you taking this precious supply of ours?"

One bee paused to say that most of the flowers wanted to be used for the good of others even if it meant giving of themselves. This was a way to help other generations come to be and would please Master Gardener tremendously.

Oh my, thought Priden. *Here we go again with pleasing Master Gardener.* He thought about all that Son had taught him in the past several weeks. Son had shared the heart of His Father with everyone. He desired that no one miss out on His message of support and care. It was as if His sole purpose was to see them all become successful and productive. How could He be so selfless? On the other hand, he, Priden, had been so obsessed with his own needs and perceived rights. Had he considered anyone else, really? Now that was a piercing question, so much so that he had to reflect on it for quite a while. Soon the little bee left to seek out another flower with more uplifted arms.

While Priden continued to ponder over this brief conversation, he began to hear a faint but growing sound. What was it? There were rich tones rolling over each other, mixing together to make a sweet harmony of what could only be… why yes, singing! No one had sung before and this presented itself as a singular act of unity and one accord that outmatched anything and everything.

Priden thought about how he did not know the words. Deep Joy noticed him as she sang with all her might. She smiled his way and motioned for him to join them.

Priden said, "What do I say? I don't know how to do this."

She stopped a moment to explain that he only needed to long to give Master Gardener and Son thanksgiving from his heart. The sound of a grateful heart would produce the words and notes to bring Them glory and honor. This would announce his portion of praise and worship for the Ones who loved him so dearly.

Priden clasped two of his leaves together and waited for something to come from within.

Deep Joy whispered, "Do you trust Him?"

"Well, yes."

"Then tell Him so, just tell Him," encouraged Deep Joy. She resumed singing but kept a partial eye on her friend hoping that he would really just let go.

Priden thought about the soakings. Wow, they had been rescued from all the drenchings, the scorchings, the insect attacks, even the changing winds. Despite it all, they were still here, still standing thanks to Master Gardener and His plans. He really had thought of everything. It was incredible how He had truly thought of *the needs* and *the wants*, but what was even more amazing was that He and His Son had thought of Priden. They knew him like no one else did. They waited for him with patience and loved him when no one else could or should. What kind of love was this, for real? Who does that? Priden knew he had done nothing to deserve such care, such unnatural love.

Just then a soft hum came from his innermost being. It slowly worked its way up and the next thing he knew, a sound came from his lips with melody in its wake. The hum kept coming and waves of gratitude swept through him releasing a soulful sound that surprised him at the same time that it made him glad.

More bees showed up to carry the tune even further. They tickled him and thanked him at the same time. He nodded slightly and continued his new song. It was a garden choir like none he had ever known. He was giving of himself for the very first time. Though it was a new experience, it was one that he hoped would continue. The bees enjoyed themselves and told him how productive he was. His nectar was sweet and the pollen was good for consumption. Priden wondered how he would have felt if he had known this moment was coming all along.

Just then, one noble bee stepped up to ask him his name. Priden obliged by giving it to him. Then the bee said that his name was Bustab. He was from a group of bees known for their productivity and long life span.

Priden noticed he was loud in his announcement and asked, "Do all of you come with a voice as robust as yours?"

Bustab said, "Well, we *are* kind of, well, loud and unashamed I reckon. We love the message we carry. It's about freedom and being real with ourselves and others."

"Well, why wouldn't you be real with everybody anyway," Priden inquired.

"Sometimes it's not acceptable to be yourself, but we have learned to not worry about what others may think of us. We just want to be at liberty to buzz the message here and there no matter what."

"Are there those who oppose your message," Priden wanted to know.

"Why sure! Not everyone understands that they have a purpose and can fulfill that purpose with the support of Son and His Father, Master Gardener. Some think they must be who they are on their own without any thought for the One who created them."

"Oh," Priden added as he remembered his own rash thoughts on the subject. He thought about saying more but dared not. *What might Bustab think of me*, Priden thought, *or maybe that's the point! What does it matter what Bustab thinks as long as I know I am at peace with myself and Master Gardener, then what else matters? Hmmm.*

"And you know, there are those who want to snuff us out entirely," continued Bustab. "They don't want us to carry the message at all!"

"What do you do then?"

"Well, it depends. If they do not mean us harm, we can pray for them. But if they try to harm us, we defend ourselves and pray all the more," replied Bustab.

"And just whyyy would you pray for those who try to harm you," inquired Priden a little surprised.

"Well, some of them just have not had time to fully understand what is going on in the grand scheme of things. They need assistance with that and mercy. They should be protected until they can gain the full realization that Master Gardener is *for* them, not *against* them."

"But what if they truly want no part of Master Gardener and His plan? What if they attack you and leave you unable to carry the message?"

"Well, I have been known to use my weapons to protect myself and present the message nonetheless." Bustab pointed to his stinger.

Priden had been noticing how odd this was. Bustab explained that his stinger was only used as a last resort for defense. Generally, he found that praying for his enemies was sufficient to change things. Sometimes, it changed the other being, but sometimes it changed his very self. No matter what, the change was always right. Prayer had a way of doing that. Priden wondered what weapon he had and asked, "So why don't I have a stinger?"

"Wow, everyone asks me that," replied Bustab. "It turns out that all have a defense because we all can pray. Didn't you know that? Haven't you tried it, Priden?"

"Well, not really. I guess I'm not sure I know what to say? And, hey who do I say it to even if I did have some idea about what to say," inquired Priden.

"Priden, you know who to speak with!" retorted Bustab. He could not believe Priden was clueless in this matter. How could anyone wonder about the *who* in this?

Priden confessed that he might know, but wanted to have some confirmation on it. He was thinking it might be that he was to reach out to a great friend, someone like Deep Joy. He might even give a quick word to Hunthir if he was still around.

Priden cleared his throat and said, "Well, I have spent a great deal of time hearing from Deep Joy. Maybe I could pray to her. She seems to love everything—trials, good times, chit chat, you know, everything. She'll listen to anything!"

Bustab looked at Priden like he was seeing upside-down flowers. Evidently, Priden needed some major help. He had been here for nearly a whole season, and yet he was practically brand new.

Thinking he should help his new friend, Bustab said, "There are three who receive our prayers. They are Master Gardener, Son, and their dear companion, Comforter. The three of them are One, and can do much about all that we share with them. The one who intercedes the most is Son. You met Him, I trust."

"Son? Why yes, I met Him. I didn't know He was so important in all this. I really can pray to Him and He will hear me?"

"Sure! He's listening to you right now, and Comforter, who is also called Holy Spirit, is with us always. They never leave us or forsake us. Isn't that great?"

Priden thought about this. *So they are not alone ever? Wow, how busy this must keep them, or better yet, how truly powerful they must be to be in all places at all times! Imagine that! They fill time and space absolutely, and are there for everyone's needs! Amazing!*

Bustab interrupted Priden's musing. "Hey friend, do you want to try to pray to them now? Just tell them you are glad they are there. They will receive it. You can't go wrong with a prayer of thanksgiving."

Priden asked if they would answer him. He wanted to know how he would know if he had gotten through to them. "Bustab, have they ever responded to your prayers before?" inquired Priden, honestly wanting to know. This seemed so far-fetched to him, but his curiosity allowed him to at least ask the question of his new acquaintance.

"Well, sometimes I have had simply a change in how I feel, you know, more peaceful and such. I might have been feeling kind of yucky before the prayer, but afterwards, I had a sense of calm that wasn't there before. Other times, I have seen a change in my circumstances that were described in the prayer. And then, Priden, sometimes there is no change at all, but I trust that they have heard me and will work on my situation at the proper time. I try not to put them in a box by telling them *what* to do or *how* to do it," Bustab concluded.

"Wow, that's scary isn't it? Just letting them decide stuff? What if a mistake is made or you don't like what they figure out is best? What then? Can you demand that they undo things? Can you refuse to do any of it, you know, just listen respectfully but then do your own thing? What do ya think," Priden asked as he came up for air.

"Now Priden, I've learned that whether the answer is *yes* or *no*, or even *no answer at all*, it always works in my favor. All three responses are given in my best interest. I just trust that things will work out well. I can't see the end from the beginning, but they can. They know what lies ahead and can prepare me for it much better than I can prepare myself. This doesn't mean that I sit around like a boulder though. No, I get up and add action to the plans they have for me. I follow the promptings of Comforter."

"Promptings of Comforter?" asks Priden in shock. "What does that mean?"

Bustab spoke up with, "It means He will lead us and guide us into the truth about everything. The truth about Heaven, the truth about Earth and the truth about all time. He's sort of an inner voice speaking to us about what happens next."

"Okay, so He tells us things that help us understand what's going on around us," Priden inquired.

"Yes! That's pretty accurate, but with one detail left out. He tells us these things with heavy doses of love. He prompts us on behalf of the Three because they care about what happens to us and they desire that none of us are lost or going astray. Isn't that just the best thing ever? I mean, really. Isn't it?" Bustab is beaming as he says this.

Priden is looking at him with real curiosity.

Bustab continues, "Priden, it's all about their love for us! They can't bear to see us fail. Even when we're making a complete mess of things, Comforter takes time to redirect us. Even if we get a little muddy in the process, He cleans us up and allows us to start afresh. How awesome is that? Ever wonder how you seem to relive some moments again and again?"

"Well, yeah, I guess I have wondered about that on occasion," replied Priden.

"Well, He's either allowing you to come to those same, or similar circumstances again, so you can rethink your response

77

to these challenges. He gives us chances to react better, and better, and better each time. Life is full of opportunities for this practice time, I must say." Bustab chuckled at this.

Priden said, "Yeah, I guess that helps us to learn from our mistakes, right?"

"Certainly, and no matter how slow we are at catching on, He always wants us to *get it* so badly that He'll allow us two chances, forty chances. Hey, however many chances it takes to perfect our thinking and our hearts," added Bustab happily.

Priden resolved that he would think about all of this, the love, the chances to become better—all of it. He thanked Bustab for stopping by and said he hoped they would see each other again.

The day continued with thoughts flitting in and out of Priden's mind. *What if this is freedom? What if I can worry less and just live more? What if Bustab is right about not being concerned about pleasing others, or even being fixed on pleasing myself? There was One to please, only One to trust. Can I do this fully?* Priden decided to try to pray. It couldn't hurt to try just this once. So looking straight ahead, he uttered these words as softly as he could, 'Son, if You and Your Father and companion, Comforter are really here for me, please show me. I want to know You.'

A cool breeze flowed over Priden's face and Priden thought he heard a sound in the breeze. He closed his eyes to listen harder. There was a sound, but not in the breeze. Where was it coming from? It was quieter than breath. This was the strangest thing, but he was not afraid in the least. A calm washed over him and then he realized that the sound was within his very self. It floated up and fell silent again. Then he knew what he had heard within! "I love you, Priden!" The words seemed to ring through him three times. Big tears he could not hold fell from his closed eyes. Love filled him and he knew beyond any doubt that he was fully in the presence of Son and His Father and Comforter. He wanted to do something—laugh, scream, cry out, anything, but all he could do was bow in stillness with tears flowing from a part of him that he didn't even know existed.

This moment became a day, then two days, and finally on the third day, Priden stepped from this perfect place and he knew he was different. He felt so *alive,* so full, so complete! He wondered how he had functioned before this experience and certainly knew that he never wanted to be without this new-found connection with the Three, especially Son. Somehow his prayer had indeed been answered! He couldn't explain how, and for the first time, it didn't matter that he had no explanation. He was...satisfied. Now all he wanted to do was give back to the One who had given so much to him.

Looking around for a place to begin, he saw the tiniest, gentlest fairy-like being. What was this? It was so beautiful with its many colors and delicate wings that wisped the air. It came closer and tickled his face. Priden knew that Deep Joy knew a lot, so he decided to check in with her.

"Deep Joy," Priden interrupted. "What is this little creature with the wings? It seems to like the food we have produced."

Deep Joy said she would consult Hunthir since this was her first time seeing these creatures as well. "Hunthir, what are these newest creatures with all the colors and tiny wings? They flit from flower to flower enjoying themselves so much!"

"Why these are butterflies! They like the nectar we produce just as the bees do. Butterflies won't hurt you. They mean no harm and we have prepared more than enough drink for them to receive. Just enjoy their company. They really brighten your day with their dancing," Hunthir explained.

Priden giggled a little when both a bee and butterfly danced together on his face. "You two are having quite a party! How are ya?" asked Priden.

"Great! We saw you last week and waited to stop by. What is your name, if it's okay to ask?" said the bee.

"Name's Priden. I've been here a long time and yes, it has taken a while for me to get to this point in, well, in my development, I guess you could say," answered Priden. "Say, what are your names? I'm so happy to meet new folk!"

"My name's Camfler," said the Bee.

"And my name's Brella," said the Butterfly.

"Wow! What awesome names! The sky is so blue today! Have you noticed? And look at those clouds! They seem extra fluffy and oh so white, almost brighter than one can bear to gaze upon. And the air is so fresh! I've never smelled anything like it! Oh my, my, my!" Priden was squealing everything.

Camfler and Brella looked at each other with quizzical looks. What was up with this guy Priden? Of course the sky looked nice and all; and the clouds were good-looking too but nothing out of the ordinary. And the air? Really? Did it smell any different than yesterday's oxygen? They waited for their new friend to calm down hoping he would do so soon.

"You two are very different, yet alike. It's pretty impressive how you can fly all over the place. I wish I could do that," replied Priden gleaming.

"It does come in handy, this flying thing, but don't covet what we are able to do. We need you to be just as you are

Priden, simply and perfectly *there*. You feed us and we feed others. We help each other create new generations of each other. It's a perfect chain of events making us a tightly-knit unit. Your foliage and flowers are glorious. We were caught by the spectacular color," said Camfler.

Brella chimed in next. "So many of your neighboring friends drew us to this part of the garden as well. They are magnificent and certainly are helping us create the new ones to come."

Priden liked both of these creatures and asked, "Will you be here tomorrow? I want you to take all that you require. I see what my purpose is now and I want to honor the One who caused me to be who I am. He is the best there is! Do you know about Son? He has a Father and Comforter who are taking care of all of us, really caring for all of this!"

"Yes, they are our most famous Friends. And you bet," they both squealed, "we'll see you bright and early tomorrow. We'll even bring you a present!" Then they all began singing the garden song. Priden sang loudest of all as he thought of tomorrow and his new friends, Camfler and Brella, but his main thoughts were of this new relationship with Son.

The next day, just as promised, Camfler and Brella flew in to visit with Priden. They brought him a special gift. It seemed to be a new form of what they called *pollen*. It was fresh and twice as fluffy as his own pollen. He welcomed the gift and thanked them for thinking of him. Then they danced and sang as if today's party had to surpass yesterday's fun.

Deep Joy heard all the ruckus and asked, "Hey Priden, what's going on over there?"

Priden said he was entertaining his new friends and he introduced Camfler and Brella to Deep Joy.

Deep Joy told Priden, "Oh yes, I met them yesterday too. They have been sprinkling doses of Son's particles on all of us. He has such a rich form to give. It comes with an anointing that is out of this world!"

Priden echoed, "Yes, totally *out of this world!*"

Just then, something totally blocked their view of the sky. However, they dismissed it and continued to party since it was a brief happening; but nearly as soon as it was gone, there it was again! This time, Priden peered upwards and saw a large T-shaped thing flying and gliding.

"What's that?" he asked Camfler.

"It's some sort of bird, Priden," she replied. "They come around looking for food too."

"Do you give them this food they are looking for," he inquired anxiously.

"Uh, no." Camfler did not want to say more. She looked to Brella wishing she could disappear. They both knew Priden would not stop questioning them until they told him the truth.

"Well, who does then? If he's come here, he must know he'll be fed here," Priden stated.

"Yes, Priden. He knows that," added Brella. She then blurted it out, "He knows *you* will feed him."

"Me? But how? Why?"

"He knows that you are mature now. You are ripe with seeds and he sees that it is time for them to be given. That's the course of life. You're all grown up now and are ready to produce the next generation."

"The next generation? Wow, this is all so mind-boggling! I was just having so much fun too!" cried Priden.

"There is great reward in being fruitful and multiplying, Priden. There will be others who will come after you and they will look like you and Son. They will speak as you do and move the same."

"Will there be many of them?" asked Priden.

"Oh yes, probably more than you can count. The bird will consume some of the seeds and many will follow after him. He will also drop many seeds and many will follow after you and Son. It's a beautiful picture of a never-ending chain of life."

Just then, the bird bowed down and nibbled at one of the seeds that had loosened during Priden's long discussion.

Priden didn't really feel a thing, just a little twinge of discomfort.

"What's your name?" he asked the bird.

"Name's Flazir. I've been watching and waiting for this meal. I thank you for preparing it for me. I never want to take anything too soon. That would not help me or you," he added and smiled.

"Will you stop by every day to do this?" Priden asked.

"Well, not every day. There are other flowers who help me and I help them. You may see some of my brothers and sisters though. They fly about the garden too," he chirped.

"Wow, I am learning so much. Even in this giving, I see that there is much good in it."

"Flazir, have you ever had this feeling? I don't know how to describe it. I guess I see that I'm a part of something bigger than me, and yet my small part is very important for all of this to flow well. It's kind of like being a tiny link in a very long chain," Priden commented.

"Yep! I know what you mean, and it makes you feel small but important all at the same time, right?"

"Yeah. Small but important," Priden echoed. "Hey, I think another seed is loosening. Go ahead, please take it. I don't want it to get lost or be wasted."

"Well, even if it fell to the ground and died, it would be revived again in practically no time at all," encouraged Flazir.

"Really!" Priden thought this was truly incredible.

"Yep. Nothing is wasted. You grew right here on this spot didn't you?"

"Well, yes," answered Priden.

"Then these seeds can do the same. There's good soil here, so no matter what, whatever you lose will prosper because of Son," explained Flazir.

"Wow!" and with that thought Priden beamed a smile and returned to his new song. For the first time, he was *content*. If his name were to be changed right now, it would have to be *Deeply Content*. Flazir flew away and the sun set on all the garden flowers as the season ran on to its end.

CHAPTER NINE

Dying: Dried and Freezing

The day opened with shivering throughout the garden. Somehow the breezes had gotten cooler in the last few weeks, but now they were consistently cold. The warmth was further away and all were suffering terribly. Priden was tempted to complain but noticed that Son was not saying a word. He saw how brittle his limbs were and all the petals were discolored now. He was *very* slumped over, but not once did He utter a word.

Priden wondered at His fortitude. How could He not scream or do something! Priden noticed that his own body was beginning to darken. His new friends were nowhere to be found. Maybe this air was too harsh for them too. He missed them. It would be nice to hear them flittering all over the place, but he no longer had anything to give them and could see how they might have moved on to perhaps another garden somewhere.

A sigh escaped his lips and Deep Joy heard him. "Priden, I know how you feel," said Deep Joy. "Just when you were set free, you now are coming to what feels like the end of things. I tell you though, what seems like the end is really a new beginning. Son will show us how this is possible. We only need to look to him. Only believe, Priden."

Priden shivered heavily and said, "I will try. He has loved me so much."

"Yes, He loves us all."

The next day brought fine white crystals that landed and stuck all over the garden—the soil, the plantings, the flowers, everything—no one was missed. Son had sunk lower and was trying to heave forward a bit, but could not do so without great effort. Time was not their friend at this point; it seemed to continue to bring the crystals. As they multiplied, they formed clumps of white masses on the flowers which had become thoroughly dry. Son was as white as the clouds and slumped even more from the weight of the crystal masses.

Priden watched Him intently and thought he heard Him say something. Was He calling on His Father, Master Gardener? He surely would know what to do. Was the powder from Him? Nonetheless, Son stood still and silent. Powder fell and fell—so unrelenting, so cold. The ice seemed to collect on Son more than anyone. It was massive and seemingly so unfair. How could anyone bear up under the weight of it all?

Priden wanted to help Him, but knew he could not. Son could not see or hear him, could he? He was so *coated*. The powder rained down without any pretense of letting up anytime soon. Indeed, this went on until the next day.

By this time, some were moaning from the cold. Many groaned because they were so tired. No one had seen anything like this before. Who was prepared for this deluge? Not one, but they all remained…waiting.

Priden checked on Son again and could not really make out where He was. It was as if He had disappeared beneath this ice blanket. Priden decided to pray his second prayer. It might help, but even if it didn't, he wanted to give it, so he said, "Son, I believe in You and I believe You are here to save us. Please save us!"

Priden saw no change. Nothing moved. All was quiet. Cold air just kept swirling around everyone. It was harsh and unrelenting, yet Priden hoped in the One who had stood by them all.

He thought, *I will trust Him. Yes, I will trust Him. No matter what, I will trust Him.*

Priden hummed a faint song of praise. Somehow it seemed to warm him. Others picked up the tune, and though it was faint, it was steady—"I will trust in the Lord."

CHAPTER TEN

Returning: Dead and Living

As day appeared, Son began to heave more; first once, then twice. With the third rise of His head, the crystal mass cracked open. With the next heave, it fell off and Priden heard these words, "It is finished!" Son bowed motionless and Priden knew He had stopped. But had he really *stopped?*

Instantly, the sky went black, blacker than Priden and the others had ever seen. It was hard to see beyond an inch or two. The white ice packs no longer even looked white, but were dingy gray. It was so frightening. Was this the doom for all of them? How could they escape this pitch black nightmare? What was happening to Son?

Just then the earth began to rumble from deep within. Earth said quietly, "Hush and do not be afraid. A great war is being waged on your behalf. The Spirit of Son is taking a great victory for all of you today, right now. Trust that all will be well. He loves you and is taking care of everything that could harm you. Dying now will not kill you forever. You'll see. You'll only sleep for a while."

"You mean we are going to be safe?" asked Priden.

"Yes, very safe. Don't worry. He has you in His heart!" replied Earth.

With one last great shaking, Earth was violently moved by Son's fight and Priden noticed that the white masses were falling from all of the garden plants. The darkness was also being pushed out of the way by a tremendous light. Everyone in the garden began cheering. Though they were dry and tired now, they cheered for joy. Darkness was gone and they had been given a marvelous light to guide them forward. Many sighed with relief. This was so welcome and they were safe just as Earth had said.

Priden looked over to see how Son was, but to his amazement, Son was no longer there! The shell of where He had been was bent and so bowed though. Priden smiled because he knew that Son had done a great thing by giving Himself to save them. The light around them became brighter and they bowed ever further in honor of that light.

Sleep wasn't long in coming. They all settled in for a time of waiting. The Light said, "I will return to receive you to Myself. I am alive forever more! Only believe in Me and never fear." Priden smiled and thought he heard a whisper, "I love you, Deeply Content." Before he could think again, he began resting in the light of his dear saving friend, Son, the most submitted flower of them all.

AFTERWORD

After choosing the sunflower as the leading character in this allegory, the author learned about its harvesting properties. *Every* portion of this flower is used for something: food, medicine, cooking oil, cosmetics, to name a few things. From the root to the flower with its seeds, every part has a purpose. The sequel to this tale will showcase Sonflower's Harvest Time message.

ABOUT THE AUTHOR

Photo by Jonalyn Gore

DeVeria Gore serves as an ordained minister at Jamestown Christian Fellowship Church, Inc. in Williamsburg, VA where they are believing God for regional, and then national revival in this final season. This book was written in an effort to capture the submitted nature of the sunflower and to demonstrate how that image showcases the submitted heart of God's Son, Jesus. It is hoped that pre-believers and believers will be drawn closer to Him.

This allegory is a fun, but sober, rendition of how pride can trick us all. When we cannot have our way, we proudly look for our own plan of escape not realizing that there is One who has the best plan already underway. This is a place the author has journeyed, a place that the Lord keeps fondly teaching her to release to Him. Also, He lovingly continues to perfect other areas in all of our lives, so this is the first of a series of books she hopes to write on the Lord's development of our character.

The author retired from public school administration after completing a 35-year career. Currently, she resides in Williamsburg, VA with husband Ed, her childhood sweetheart. The Lord gave them Open Door Ministries to bless others with the word and worship. To date, they have ministered in England and the U.S. She also provides diversity training for organizations. They have an awesome son and daughter-in-law and a fabulous daughter and son-in-law. Five wonderful grand-children keep them young and excited about life!

CPSIA information can be obtained
at www.ICGtesting.com
Printed in the USA
BVOW11s0758020518
515048BV00001B/108/P